Reycraft Books
55 Fifth Avenue
New York, NY 10003

Reycraftbooks.com

Reycraft Books is a trade imprint and trademark of Newmark Learning, LLC.

This edition is published by arrangement with China Children's Press & Publication Group, China.
© China Children's Press & Publication Group

Library of Congress Cataloging-in-Publication Data is available.

ISBN: 978-1-4788-6871-2

Printed in Guangzhou, China
4401/0919/CA21901490

10 9 8 7 6 5 4 3 2 1

First Edition Paperback published by Reycraft Books 2019

Reycraft Books and Newmark Learning, LLC support diversity and the First Amendment,
and celebrate the right to read.

REYCRAFT
BOOKS

I AM HUA MULAN

BY QIN WENJUN

ILLUSTRATED BY YU RONG

In my dream I am dressed as a warrior.

I have long eyelashes.

My hair ribbons flutter in the breeze.

When I draw my dream, I see her...

I see Hua Mulan.

The Hua family lived over 1,500 years ago. Mulan's sister was a new bride. Her brother was a lively little boy. They were a **happy** family.

Mulan read old books on
the art of war,
sometimes all afternoon.

Mulan's father taught her the skills of a warrior.

She learned to ride,
to use a bow and arrow,
to **fight** with a spear.

As soon as she was old enough, Mulan looked after

the horses, grazed the sheep, and went hunting.

But every year the
Rouran came raiding.

The Rouran chief led his people

southward from the steppes.

More men were needed at the front.

A list of names was drawn up. On the list
was Hua Hu, Mulan's father.

But Mulan's father was not in good health.

How could he fight?

Mulan decided she would go in his place.
She tried every which way to persuade him.
Eventually father and daughter agreed to
a duel. Whoever won would join the army.

Mulan's skills were stunning.
She was clever.

And ...

she won!

She went to the East Market to choose a

fast horse,

to the West Market to fit a

good saddle,

to the South Market to buy

warrior's clothes,

and to the North Market to find a

sharp spear.

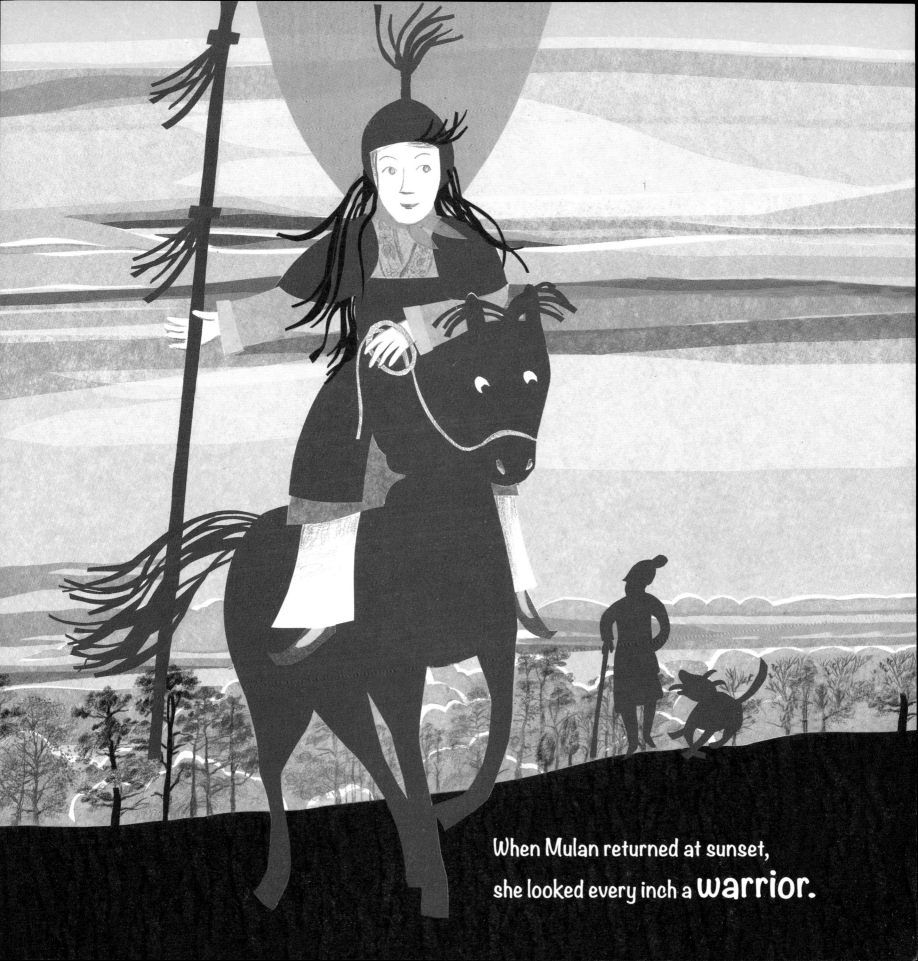

When Mulan returned at sunset,
she looked every inch a **warrior.**

On her last day at home,

her heart filled with

sadness,

Mulan planted peonies

in front of the house.

The day came.

Mulan the Warrior set out with her horse.

That night, she lay on the soft clay ground

and rested her head on her hard silver sword.

The earth was her bed.
The sky was her cover.

The commanders signed in the new soldiers and horses. The troops **grew in might.**

They galloped hundreds of miles in the light of day. When evening fell, they slept at the foot of Slay Tiger Mountain.

As dawn broke, the marauding enemy arrived. The quiet camp instantly became a battleground. The commander led the charge. Mulan leapt on her horse, her spear at the ready, and followed.

But the enemy broke free.

The commander wanted victory, and gave orders to pursue and kill. The troops fell straight into the enemy's trap.

Mulan was brave.

She attacked the enemy and rescued the commander.

Years passed. Mulan fought a hundred battles. She impressed the commander with her strength and daring. The warriors did not know she was a girl, and begged Brother Mulan to teach them how to attack, to fight with a sword, to bend their bows and shoot eagles. They were her Iron Brothers.

Late one night, when Mulan was on guard duty, she noticed something startling the birds. They took flight and headed south. She watched them for a while and discovered the enemy lying in wait, preparing to launch a raid.

But when the enemy soldiers finally
crept into the camp, **they found it empty!**
Mulan had reported the enemy position, and the commander
had devised a plan—to divide the troops and surround the enemy.
Mulan led the charge. The warriors stormed the enemy camp.

The enemy soldiers were under attack.

They could not retreat.

They fled in fear.

Mulan galloped ahead to block their way. She captured the man

in front, who wore lion-skin trousers and boots up to his knees.

The enemy's leader!

All of a sudden,

Mulan fell from her horse.

She had been shot in the arm but had ignored it

until she could no longer fight.

Finally, the overpowered enemy surrendered.

The battle was won!

The cheers of victory from the commander and the generals rang out so loud that the clouds parted at the noise.

But still the war raged on.

Whenever her arm hurt,

Mulan would look at her reflection in the river.

As she combed her long hair, she would think

of her family and the peonies she had planted.

The Iron Brothers wanted to help, but Mulan sent them away. She saw to the wound, bandaged her arm, and washed her clothes all by herself.

At last, the war ended.
Victory!

The generals waited in camp to receive their medals.

But Mulan couldn't wait.

She shot home like an arrow. She had been away for twelve years. When her mother and father and sister and brother heard her voice, they came running out to greet her. Could this valiant warrior really be her?

Mulan took off her helmet. She saw her family and the gorgeous peonies growing around the house.

They **hugged** and **hugged.**

The tears flowed. The most precious peony of all had come home!

Now life was peaceful and easy. Mulan planted flowers, wove cloth, and wore beautiful clothes. The family lived happily.

One day, the Iron Brothers

came to visit Mulan. But she hid and told her little brother to chat and have fun with them. They never knew that their Brother Mulan, who had fought with them on the battlefield and earned so many medals, was a woman.

I don't have impressive warrior's clothes. I don't need to fight instead of my father. But I am strong. And I'm proud of being a girl!

My friends gave me the best nickname. They call me Mulan!

I am Hua Mulan!

QIN WENJUN

The author of many popular children's books, Qin Wenjun is also vice president of the Shanghai Writers' Association. She has won many awards for her books, including the prestigious Children's Literature Award from the Chinese Writers' Association.

YU RONG

Award-winning illustrator Yu Rong first trained as a teacher, before turning her attention to art and earning an MA from the Royal College of Art in London. Her illustrations have been published in many books worldwide.